The Toothless Puppy

To Campbell and Wilco, who fill our hearts every day.

Published by Dog Haus Publishing, Seattle
www.doghauspublishing.com

Edited and Designed by Girl Friday Productions
www.girlfridayproductions.com

Illustrations by Agung Nurhidayat

Interior and Cover Design by Rachel Christenson
Cover Illustration by Agung Nurhidayat

ISBN-13: 978-0-9982439-0-0
ISBN-10: 0-9982439-0-6
e-ISBN: 978-0-9982439-1-7

Library of Congress Control Number: 2016917576

First Edition

Printed in the United States of America

The Toothless Puppy

A Tale of Differences

By Karen Almon and Ashley Almon

DOG HAUS PUBLISHING

Campbell the golden retriever is a happy-go-lucky puppy. Every day her mommy takes her to the park, where she swims, runs, and plays.

When she comes home, Campbell is always exhausted from playing with the other dogs in the park. After eating her dinner and taking a sip of water, she curls up on her bed and slowly drifts off to sleep, a very happy dog.

One morning, while lapping up some water from her dish, she suddenly catches a glimpse of her reflection and notices she is missing a tooth. "That's strange," she says. "When did that happen?" Campbell is surprised and upset. "Why don't I have a tooth where other dogs do?" she wonders. "Did I lose my tooth somewhere? Or is there something wrong with me?"

Campbell tries to go about her day, doing the things that make her happy, but something is wrong now. She can't stop thinking about her missing tooth. Where did it go? Could she find it and put it back? She doesn't like feeling different. She is worried about what the other dogs might think of her. She wants to be accepted. Why can't she be like the other dogs she knows? They have all their teeth!

Maybe someone has seen it somewhere, thinks Campbell. She slips out the door and starts down her favorite path, searching for someone to help her find her tooth.

Before long, she runs into her friend Hudson, an enormous golden doodle, who is playing in the yard with his favorite red ball.

"Hudson, I am missing a tooth!" cries Campbell.

Hudson looks up at his friend, cocking his head to the side and flipping his long hair out of his eyes. "So you are!" Hudson says when he can see properly.

"But why am I missing a tooth, while you have all of yours? Where did mine go? Why am I different from everyone else?" asks Campbell.

"It's OK to be different, Campbell," Hudson replies. "Look at me—my hair is so long, it covers my eyes! But that's OK; it doesn't make me cry."

You are who you are, and that's the truth!
You are who you are, and you don't need proof.

Campbell thanks Hudson, but she is not convinced. Without her front tooth, she still feels different from the other dogs. *Hudson might be different, too,* she thinks, *but at least he still looks like other dogs when he smiles.* As Hudson runs off to play with his ball, Campbell continues her journey.

From afar, Campbell sees another friend, Annabelle the pony. Campbell props her paws on top of Annabelle's fence, and the pony trots over.

"Annabelle, have you seen my tooth?" Campbell asks.

Annabelle neighs and shakes her head. "It's not here," she says.

Campbell sighs. "Without a front tooth, I look so different from other dogs. I'm afraid that no one will like me because of it."

Annabelle looks at Campbell with kindness. "Look at me, Campbell—I am missing a shoe! But I don't care; it doesn't make me blue."

You are who you are, and that's the truth!
You are who you are, and you don't need proof.

Campbell gives Annabelle a bark of thanks and continues down the road, still hoping to find her tooth somewhere along the way.

Campbell sees her friend Wilco in a distant field. He is herding sheep. Once the sheep are grazing peacefully in their pasture, Wilco comes running over to say hello.

"Wilco, I'm missing a tooth! Have you seen it anywhere?"

"No, I haven't," replies Wilco. "Did you lose it?"

"I don't know," admits Campbell. "But I feel different without it. I'm not like other dogs."

"I know all about being different," Wilco says. "Look at me—I am minus a tail! But I don't care; I can't fail."

You are who you are, and that's the truth!
You are who you are, and you don't need proof.

Although she knows her friends are trying to help, Campbell is still unhappy about her missing tooth. She wishes that there wasn't something different about her. She feels like she might cry.

"Oh, Campbell," says Wilco. "Don't worry! Come with me—I've got some things to show you."

Wilco leads Campbell down a path into the forest.

"Where are we going?" asks Campbell.

"You'll see!" says Wilco. "We're going to meet some other animals who are different, too."

After a while, Wilco and Campbell arrive at a pond, where a pair of ducks are teaching their ducklings to swim.

Wilco points to the ducks. "See, Campbell? Ducks don't have any teeth, and it doesn't bother them!"

You are who you are, and that's the truth!
You are who you are, and you don't need proof.

"I don't know, Wilco," says Campbell. "The ducks might not have teeth, but they're still like other birds. Without my tooth, I feel so different from other dogs."

"Come with me," says Wilco. "I have more to show you!"

They walk a bit farther and slip through a gate and into a nearby bird sanctuary. Close by, they notice the penguins frolicking about in their cold, icy habitat.

"See, Campbell?" asks Wilco. "Penguins are birds, and they can't fly. But they can swim and dive and are *awesome* anyway!"

You are who you are, and that's the truth!
You are who you are, and you don't need proof.

Campbell nods thoughtfully, but she can't shake her sadness. She needs a hug from the people who love her most. "Thank you for being such a good friend, Wilco, but I think I just want to go home now."

"I understand," says Wilco. "But remember—no one is perfect. We love you no matter what. Tooth or no tooth."

As Campbell wanders home, her thoughts turn to all the animals she saw on her journey who have their own differences. There's Hudson the golden doodle, who has so much hair over his eyes that he can't see. There's Annabelle the pony, who is missing a shoe, and Wilco the sheepdog, who doesn't have a tail where other dogs do. She remembers the ducks who don't have teeth and the penguins who can't fly. So why does she still feel sad and confused?

When she arrives home, she is excited to see her daddy, who greets her with a big hug.

"What's wrong Campbell?" he asks. "Why so sad?"

"Daddy, today I noticed I am missing a tooth," she says. "Where did it go? Why am I different?"

Daddy gives her a cuddle and says gently, "You have always been missing a tooth. You were born that way. It's never changed the way we feel about you. Missing a tooth doesn't make you any less perfect. It makes you unique!"

You are who you are, and some things you can't change. You are one of a kind, and we love you just the same!

Campbell finally understands the lesson Wilco was trying to teach her: it's OK to be different. It's what makes us who we are! Being different is the one thing everyone has in common.

Campbell gives her daddy another big hug and trots into the house, excited to see her special reflection in the water bowl again.

You are who you are, and that's the truth.
You are who you are, and you don't need proof.

The End

Acknowledgments

We would like to thank Girl Friday Productions for their professionalism and acute attention to detail. They successfully guided us through our first self-publishing experience, making it informative and fun! We are grateful to Emilie Sandoz-Voyer, our editor, who held our hand the entire way. Her suggestions and comments enriched and rounded out the story line.

About the Authors

Karen Almon was born and raised in Seattle and earned her bachelor's degree in education from Washington State University. She worked as an elementary school teacher for five years, and between teaching and raising a daughter of her own, Karen's love and appreciation for children's books grew. She was inspired to write this book by her former students and her family's real-life canine companions, Campbell and Wilco, and she has teamed up with her daughter, Ashley, to make *The Toothless Puppy* a reality.

Ashley Almon, an artist and true dog lover, has a bachelor's degree in comparative literature and film and media studies from the University of Washington. Before graduating, her passion for literature and children took her all the way to India, where she taught English and writing at the Prema Vasam orphanage. In her spare time, Ashley participates in Seattle's local theater scene as both a director of children's plays and an actress in multiple shows per year. She currently works as a writer for an international travel blog and also acts as vice chair for the Northwest Art Project for Seattle Public Schools through the Junior League of Seattle.

CPSIA information can be obtained at www.ICGtesting.com
Printed in the USA
LVIW01n2259040417
529650LV00002B/6